THE FUTURE ROOM

4 Fairytales for Adults

STAVO MUSTANG CRAFT

BY THE MUSES PRESS

Table of Contents

Preface: The Future Is Now

This 30th ANNIVERSARY EDITION of "The Future Room" marks its First Official Printing for public consumption. I believe this release (finally!) will provide the dozens of people who have kept those original, free, inkjet-printed copies —or framed illustrations— on their shelves for all these years, a cause for celebration. An old friend revived!

A 30-year gap between creation and release garners an edge of mystery in itself. But it must be understood that these illustrated stories were primarily created as companion pieces for musical projects. Two of the four stories (*The Future Room, A World of Aliens*) specifically arrived on Earth in 1996 & 1999, with another (*The Beauty Bomb*) joining 10 years after *TFR,* expanding on Galexia's legend. These served as components of a new kind of concept album, where the supporting themes behind the lyrical content of songs, was given a more intricate back story. But one only hinted at in spoken snippets added to and between songs, both for recordings and live performance. Video clip examples are shared for this special edition in the *Postlude... A Time Capsule.*

That might explain the presence of a certain mirroring at times: of themes, of occurrences, of characters. This is something I will call "Residual Haunting" because the term *motif* doesn't quite articulate it for me.

With these stories finally telling their OWN independent tale for the first time, their original purpose for existing has become part of their character. In editing them to stand as interwoven worlds, the "residual haunting" became evident to me. Even how the first story *ends* with walking up the stairs, as the last story *begins* with a traversing up a waterfall... they mirror each other, wink at each other, play inter-dimensional feng shui together.

As the unified stories told me who they were, and not vice-versa, it recalled for me Joseph Campbell's *Hero With a Thousand Faces*, exploring how myths repeat certain archetypal arcs, with different external characters and situations. Let's say *Residual Haunting* then, is when a 'ghost' person, thing, plotline, creature, phrase, or event is recurring, almost as a deju vu for emphasis. I remember being thrilled by avant-garde playwright & director Richard Foreman's experimental performances at the Ontological-Hysteric Theater in New York City, and how phrases and sequences (or just numbers) would repeat, like you were revisiting a thought or time in your mind, even if it were just a time from 5 minutes ago. Or how Jean-Luc Godard in his New Wave classic, *Alphaville,* used repeating visual symbols, phrases ("voice of a pretty sphinx"), sounds, and scenes that set a dream-tinged quality, but specifically to announce, in a sense, that there is a search for meaning happening here. A ruminating.

In the final edit, it was clear that this is essentially one book, told in 4 parts, about the revaluing —and power of— the inner world. Or at the least, an attempt to make one artwork from 4 like-spirited elements. Which led me to consider how they each embodied the 4 classical elements of air, fire, earth, and water. Some traditions also name a fifth element of ether/space, and upon reflection, it seemed the reader of the book (the watcher) is that fifth element.

My art journey really does begin with *The Future Room*. Not just a story, but my own "artist persona origin story" lived and honed into being from the six years that proceeded it, of journaling, writing songs, dressing crazily, following my fascinations and teaching myself the universe, in my own language. It declared my sense of creative mission and identity. It's still my blueprint.

And in a delightful irony, the entire idea behind my creations of that period was a 'message in a bottle' approach, where I had no intention of doing promotion, touring, finding a label or manager, or pursuing what some valued as fame. I valued creating and new experiences. So it was *consciously* about making artifacts/objects in the PRESENT, intending to be discovered/excavated IN THE FUTURE, as an unearthed archeological finding from the PAST. And today, here it is manifesting that original intention, "rising from the oceans" 30 years later. Life imitates art... a true residual haunting.

For James Broughton....

I sent the experimental filmmaker & poet James Broughton
a copy of "The Future Room" 30 years ago, and stunningly
he wrote back, "I see the future has arrived and you have the
biggest room in it. Fabulous, all the way!" ~ a correspondence
which he sent with a feather.

Still the most dear note I have received. This is for you, Jimmy.

AIR.

THE FUTURE ROOM

1:5 - "tHE fUTURIST fROM iNNER-sPACE"

Some fairytales are real. Much in the same way that what seems most real is often false. And how sometimes the messenger who awakens you out of the sleep of life, and into your true dreams, comes from someplace previously unseen; almost invisible to you, until the very moment you meet.

Where he was from —outerspace or innerspace, the past or the future, or whether his present was perhaps a Dimension of Places Tomorrow— who could say?

"I feel very closely associated with colour," he offered, kicking his walking stick high up into the air, as if testing the wind, to discover the hidden directions of the future.

"You see, when I want to express my deepest strength and beauty, I seek always to radiate a vast array of brilliant colour. A different approach, you might say, to displaying a sense of power."

"Like a peacock," the Priest of earthPresent quipped. "King of the beasts."

"I place anything that illuminates toward the top," The Futurist replied. "Of course, where I'm from, things are very different from here," he continued. A light shone from the centre of his hand. "But then our eyes are not like yours. We can see intentions."

"Now that particular skill," the Priest of earthPresent thought aloud, "would be quite useful for my purposes." He trickling his finger down to meet his sword. "These are not times of conversation, after all... but of Conquest."

"And yet," The Futurist challenged, "it's always the first person to raise a fist, who has lost the argument." This caused the Priest to stop in his wandering for a moment and turn his head, finally catching a slight start from the Futurist's palm and its unfamiliar effusing.

"The Futurist Walks Though the
Walls in his Mind"

"Something that appears one way," The Futurist concluded, "but which is, in fact, another... A show of strength, that is Not." He began humming and almost immediately took to a brief waltz, gardening his imaginary plants. "Unlike a peacock," he teased.

His hands moved in caressing motions as if speaking through his fingers. The Priest of earthPresent watched him with curiosity, but would not be distracted from his own point of reference.

"Your world runs by a different Order," the Priest acknowledged, with a weary brow raised. He fumbled for his hidden wallet in a sudden panic that it might be missing, but found it resting calmly in his hip pouch. When he looked up, The Futurist was gone from sight. Turning around, he saw the space traveler begin to glow.

The Futurist closed his eyes. And a moment later, became a stone.

"There is far more in heaven and earthPresent than in even your wildest imagination," his voice echoed. "Likewise, there is more to you. Much more than you now see." The rock radiated. "Even beyond your Human Trappings."

"H u m a n Trappings? What more is there to us than that?" demanded the Priest, becoming agitated by The Futurist's uncanny convictions. "Flesh and blood is what we are!" The Priest rubbed his hands, as if proving that reality was truly as it appeared to him. "We are real, not fantasie."

The Futurist peeled with a laughter almost eerie in its lightness. He was coy and self-contained; a riddler with flirtatious leanings. His eyes were the colour of a clear noon-day sky with a centre, the colour of midnight.

"My friend, you will never be real until you can live your fantasie. It is the most truthful part about you," The Futurist flatly spoke. Then he chuckled again, as if finding a humorous tidbit amidst his invisible novels. "Until fantasie is real for you, you have accepted far too little of reality."

"Granted, your vision is irregular," the Priest of earthPresent returned. "But on this planet, where you now stand, people are put away in very tight coats for beliefs a tad less eccentric than yours!"

The Futurist seemed to be paying little attention to the Priest's objections, retaking his original form while dandyishly beholding his own reflection in his hand. "Mind your assumptions," he said very quietly, as if telling a secret naughtily ahead of its time. "Your planet has not accepted enough of what constitutes Reality to qualify as Sane, yet." He paused before adding, "That will take some doing."

The Priest of earthPresent looked out into the Vast. He saw far into the distance, what looked to be a runway of white roof shingles. Then one moved. And then three...into the sky. He saw the shingles had been birds.

"And if that be so," The Futurist interrupted his thoughts, "perhaps the stars in the sky..." and he paused dramatically, shifting his walking stick upwards, "are actually just people...wearing lights on their hats."

*"The Stars are just people wearing
lights on their hats"*

A tall hat encircled his spiral-inspired head, with flashing stars which disappeared by the time the Priest finished blinking. In fact, it happened so quickly, he wasn't sure he had truly seen the queer signal his eyes had sent him at all.

"Nonsense!" the Priest insisted, startled; but more confident that his own life was not comprised of misbegotten illusions. It was shaking to a man's faith in the limitations he had so taken for granted, to watch The Futurist toss reality about like a cat's toy. Perhaps the roof was truly coming off the house, he began to think.

"On my planet, our eyes are different than yours," The Futurist reminded.

"Are you not on my planet, now?" the Priest inquired. "Where the stars are not just people…"

The Futurist didn't respond, but with his eyes and his knowing, neither of which the Priest could properly decipher. Then, The Futurist took on a tone of boredom. "It must be difficult living in such a non-conceptual world."

Three paces later, The Futurist's cape had turned in colour, from a hazy purple to a metallic silver. The Priest felt a little overwhelmed, for sure.

This Futurist was a kind of madman who was not mad at all. Not using conventional standards, anyway. Reality was conforming to his whims. Or so it seemed. And what did this madman—if he be man, at all—want from earthPresent; he whose own world was so far Beyond?

"Let's approach this another way," The Futurist suggested thoughtfully, now munching on a handful of something the Priest might as well have believed to be The Futurist's private storehouse of fantasie-dust. "What would it mean to you now, to be truly alive?"

"To make it to the next day, of course," the Priest affirmed. "We are here, concerned with problems of survival."

"In effect, You Are Your Eyes," said The Futurist's ghostly apparition, "and choosing as your own, the vision of the blind." His silhouette walked like water toward the Priest, and as his hands touched the Priest's head, I also felt hands upon my own head. It was then that I realized I was more than just myself, but were in some way, two.

"Listen with your fingers, and tell me what they can see..." he demanded. I didn't want to answer. Didn't want to follow where he was leading. His palm upon my head was itself a vision. "Can you perceive, even what's right in front of you?" he asked.

"I can," I somehow murmured.

"What are you, then?"

I felt the ground with my fingers and shook. I wanted more than ever to avoid The Futurist's questions. An army I would have gladly fought, but a mirror? Oh, to be conquered by such an Intimate Gesture.

"Flesh and blood," I stammered.

"Can we be any more of Nothing than that?" he called, as if enraged at the suggestion. "Beyond that, please!"

I sought to escape and felt myself levitating. Hovering above, from outside my body, I watched The Futurist caressing the Priest's head.

"Our earliest ancestors?" the Priest shrieked, "the Common Tree Shrew!"

"You crazy bird," The Futurist cackled. "Stones and minerals are closer to your earliest ancestors, but what can I expect from you? You've been told these things...."

The Futurist forcefully began reciting something, and then added, "Your people once firmly believed that this planet was flat, because they were also quick to be deceived by appearances."

I understood what he meant when he spoke. But, really, I was still basking in the waves of, what I can only describe to you as thought, sent forth from The Futurist's fingers like some deranged yet master pianist, whose songs were like miniature paintings. I had no response to offer. Only a faint sense of wonder, mostly at why he was here.

"There are too many Priests of whole worlds who don't even acknowledge their invisible reality," The Futurist said. "Once you can admit to yourself that it exists," he continued, adding a delicate pause...surely for dramatic effect, "you will inevitable find that there is more...."

When I looked up at The Futurist to grasp his meaning, I saw not what I had expected to see...or had ever expected to see. But the sight before me explained beyond words what he had meant.

The Unicorn barely moved, but her eyes held spiraling universes deeper woven than the very fabric of Time. It appeared as though the sky around her were melting, as if barely deciding to exist.

"No," said the voice of The Futurist from within the strange white apparition, "I, too, am not as I appear. But this illusion will suffice."

"You are You," I stammered.

"And What Be That?" she replied from within her formlessness. "What form would be true? One gradation further into the melting sky, and I would exist here without any form at all, in that mysterious realm which you so fear and call death."

"Death?" I muttered barely audible even to myself.

"The Unicorn exists in a Dimension of Now..."

The Unicorn laughed without laughing and said, "That concept shall be your final illusion."

The Futurist stood before me like before, now extending his arm toward the bank of trees ahead. Their colour was reminiscent of fall, yet the smell in the air was distinctly spring. Perhaps both were true for me. The mask of all I had believed about the world, and about myself, was peeling.

As I motioned to stand, I felt as if I were waking from a dream and was somehow transported to a completely different place, even though our conversation and the happenings of the day felt fluid. The Unicorn's form was gone now, though I would hesitate to say that for certain.

Upon hearing me, The Futurist laughed, and for the first time, I did not feel mocked by his laughter, but felt instead a greater sense of ease.

2:5 - "tHE wILDERNESS oF cONSCIOUSNESS"

As I entered the forest, my feelings were like imprints on some abstract canvas which, when I tried to perceive them, only dropped further out of the zone of my experience, existing just out of sight...perhaps, somewhere in that melting sky, of which the Unicorn had spoken.

"It is impossible to see yourself on the canvas when you are that very canvas," The Futurist said in his unusual manner. "This wilderness which grows all around you is not the kind with gnats that eat at your flesh, or buffalo roaming the open fields. It is, rather, the wilderness of consciousness." He extended his arms as if an intergalactic airline steward showing off the dimensions of a spacecraft.

"It is a space craft, if you will," he continued, "a self-generating environment composed of your own...well, inner-space."

"Is this for real?" the Priest of earthPresent asked me.

"At this point, I'm just observing, too," I answered, "but we know we're Some-Where."

The Priest and I were aware of each other, though we couldn't see each other. I could only surmise that we were one and the same, since The Futurist had assured us we were in our own inner-space, and there was no separation between us.

Being in this state of disembodiment was a lesson for both of us in accepting the existence of the Invisible World. Nothing was for certain, however, if you understand my position. Even The Futurist was, himself, perhaps no more than a holographic transmission from who knows where.

The Futurist clasped his hands together, gaining friction as he rubbed, and slowly pulled his fingers apart as though he were sculpting energy into a ball. For what purpose, I couldn't guess. After a brief pause, he held it out to me, and I felt the Priest of earthPresent reach out to receive the charged sphere.

"The Futurist looks out at the Wilderness of Consciousness from his Oversized Windows"

It was exhilarating to touch, and though I couldn't see it, it is true that I was acutely aware of its existence. Once I actually held the sphere in my hands, I was sure enough it was some incarnation of night and day, and communicated this silently to the Priest.

"Yin-Yang," the Priest said, breathing a little heavy from the weight of his uncertainties. I tried to soothe him, but in a strange way, he was on his own.

"Very good," The Futurist remarked, seeming genuinely pleased. "The circle you now hold is the springboard from which all material things take their image." He kicked his walking stick very high into the air, and pressed down upon the ground as if making a point to the soil, which, admittedly, was made of consciousness. His actions were beginning to take on new meaning to me wherever we were, and because everything he did communicated some form of understanding, I trusted more freely in what he said, and that we had somehow left what I knew as earthPresent.

"Traveling to other planes, like traveling from one day to the next, is all simply a matter of fluidity," The Futurist said, continuing to respond to both thoughts and words, once again blurring the distinction for the Priest and I between the external and internal. And somehow this ball of energy that the Priest held was reinforcing this feeling. More and more, there literally was no solid ground.

"In the world of the mind, there is no solid ground," The Futurist's voice could be heard, though I could no longer see him. "All is flux and balance. Welcome to my planet, where we all walk on water."

"This world of consciousness is the planet of which you spoke?" the Priest asked, finally easing his breath. It is a curious paradox, but somehow the knowledge of being in flux was somehow soothing in a way that felt very much like solid ground. For the Priest, it was a matter of finally realizing where he stood.

"Yes, yes," the Unicorn assured us, sounding much more light hearted, perhaps because she was back in her forest. "Now, bring the orb's energy into your Self. Don't be surprised if you feel movement, a dancing..."

Everything became strangely amorphous, and my vision was impaired or at least altered. I saw mostly spirals of light, spirals of green.

"Why am I not seeing you, Futurist?" the Priest asked.

"You have not yet given yourself over to Nevermore," he replied. "You'll move higher into the Sky Planes by going further Inward. As you Trust, I will become more apparent to your eyes."

I closed my eyes to once again stop relying on them. First, I felt the unifying ball of energy within my nervous system. And as I stilled my mind, it occurred to me that my own bloodstream was somehow linked to a great cosmic river that flowed like roots, connecting every human life... stemming from the Beginnings of Time.

When I felt at peace, I opened my eyes to see if I had arrived in Nevermore. Everything was blurry, and light began filling what I had thought were physical spaces. This was most frightening because, believing fully in the existence of the physical world, this light penetrated my deepest beliefs.

I kept hearing the Priest thinking "Is this not death? Is this not death?" and I wanted to hold on to the world I knew, yet felt the promise of a world that still would exist, from where the Unicorn was speaking to me. Her words varied in tone between distinguishably male and female, older and younger, and yet, none of these audible sounds made any direct sense. They did not require translation.

"I saw mostly Spirals of Light, Spirals of Green..."

Then I began to be older and younger myself. I began to be woman and man, yin and yang. The Priest extended his arms perfectly sideways to release our resistance to this overwhelming flow of energy. The only solace seemed to be in submission. It was not submitting exactly, but giving way to aspects that contained everything. A sensation like a pulse began beating at the centre of my forehead, and I thought I must be getting closer to the Unicorn.

"YES!" the Priest screamed, without knowing why.

The Futurist sighed with a fond sense of remembrance, "You don't need to know about that just yet." He extended what looked to be a glass of wine, and smiled politely.

The Priest of earthPresent starred at the extended glass of wine transfixed. He reached into his hip pouch, and fumbling, grabbed his pen and small note pad. These pages carried his thoughts, his grocery lists, his scribblings, which all seemed from another world now. Putting pen to paper, he wrote the word "YES" as if it contained the most gravely important key to existence.

"Gladly," the Priest of earthPresent recovered, taking the glass from The Futurist with an unsteady hand, and slipping the note pad back into his pouch. He needed a drink, if only to convince him that the place he was in was, by all accounts, real. The glass was real. And yes, the wine... divinely so.

I also knew we were in The Futurist's home, which was decorated as individualistically as his attire. Colors I didn't even know existed floated around the room like incredibly large, visible molecules.

These uncommon balls were somehow configurations of light and emitted subtle vibrations that I could feel when I walked near them, as if they were planets being interrupted by a passing meteor. The orbs usually hovered, but occasionally took on an air of having conscious intention as they would suddenly shift air space and hover someplace else. The Futurist assured me that my perception of movement was an illusion. I wasn't sure whether he was limiting that statement to these balls of light or not.

There was an amazing amount of glistening within everything, in fact. And looking out at the forest from his oversized windows, I could see that there was no shortage of light in the natural world of consciousness, as I should have supposed. Looking around the room, there were many doors which were all opened, and which, from my vantage point, led down immensely long, infinite hallways, with the dislodged doors extended all the way down. It was like a reflection of a reflection of a reflection.

The Futurist smiled at my musings of thought. This much was clear to me, as were many things on this planet of transparency. I began to understand some of his earlier references to the place he "came from."

After a few sips of his divine wine, my physical self, the Priest of earthPresent, was able to sit down in an unimaginably soft yet sturdy chair, and discuss matters of great consequence without words. Although talk could be discarded here, we enjoyed looking into each other's eyes, and sharing a warm smile, all for their own sake, as the conversation of thought went on.

Through this time, I came to understand some miraculous things.

"The glass was Real...and the Wine, Divinely so..."

Firstly, music was ever-present on The Futurist's planet, and perhaps this accounted for his whimsical disposition. The impression that he always wanted to burst into song was not so far from the truth. For, in actually, I learned, he was a song. And so was I and everything else.

I would have resisted the notion, I suppose, if I had not directly been experiencing that feeling on this strange planet... of floating... but from within the mind, as if riding the wave of some enchanted melody. And it was obvious to me more then, than now, that everything which seems so separate from us is woven together, not "like" relationships between harmonies, but exactly so.

I also came to understand that within myself were greater and greater variations of separated yet connected selfhood. The Priest of earthPresent and I were not simply of the same Being, but, like outer and inner, constituted a kind of sacred marriage between the "I" and "me" of the Self. The Futurist communicated to us that direct, conscious awareness of this marriage would be of the utmost importance on our journey through our own "inner fluidity," which, once we returned to earthPresent, would simply be as a rambling river dreamsong within our veins, like a melody buoyant beyond physical space, in the likeness of the melting sky.

Though this river is eternal, The Futurist still assured me he would meet me when I reached its end. When I asked how he knew I would make it, he replied that I already had, and he said it with the kind of conviction that only The Futurist could have, and with a warmth that made me believe my marriage to the Priest was not my last. Together, the Priest and I, as one, would unite with yet another, and I knew that somehow The Futurist was intimately involved.

3:5 - "tHE mIND cAMERA"

Dreams are much closer to Reality than daily living on earthPresent. In the physical planes, things are very clumsy, inflexible, and primitive. A toaster becomes a toaster. A clock seems no longer a symbol. The workings of reality become dependent on lazy, stubborn exactitude. But also, things become crystallized... slowing down so they can really be touched.

The Priest picked up the ornately covered volume that lay on the floor of his new surroundings. It was a text of old writings from the times on earthPresent when they still used words to communicate. It told of the times of civic slavery when the social order was built around exploitation rather than floatation, living in a cage instead of being a sage. It told of the times when people thought salvation came from outside themselves in the form of another, rather than recognizing their savior as states of mind available to themselves. It told of The Grand Delusion that had led people to believe the world was physical at its core, rather than psychodynamic. It all seemed so far away, now. It truly was ancient history.

He put the book down, shivering a bit from the chill he felt reviewing his own past, in a world where he had been so deceived by appearances.

The room he found himself in now seemed almost Void of Past. It was new. The wall was bare except for a single word somehow painted yet hovering that simply read "BECOME."

The Priest was aware that his mental shifts were such that physical reality could no longer support his previous world. He was like an alien who had lost his own planet and was forced to forge a whole new concept in living. In a very real way, the Priest's planet, earthPresent, was no more. Home was simply wherever he was. Which was not such a bad place to be, he thought. Maybe he liked it better than before. He didn't even recognize the fact that seeing the sky from here would have been impossible on earthPresent, considering this room didn't really have an "Outside" to speak of.

"The Priest considers Escaping the Future through a hole in his Mind..."

"You are learning quickly," The Futurist said, greeting him by walking through the other end of the wall.

"Fancy meeting you here," the Priest said.

The Futurist laughed. "Where else?"

"I'm beginning to wonder," he replied.

The Futurist snapped his fingers, and long paintbrushes, still wet with paint, appeared within his reach. He looked up at the wall, as if pondering how he might raise the entire scope of his future in a flurry of firm, committed strokes.

"What are you doing now?" the Priest asked.

"I paint my own reality," The Futurist quipped with little kidding. "Move...a step to the side..."

I couldn't move.

In any voyager's travels, there comes a time when someone must come along and introduce a new landscape; to make clear where the voyager is standing on that spiraling canvas of reality, so that he might understand where to take the next step. Perhaps this was the reason for the appearance of this curious visitor to my lonely planet.

"You're making an inter-dimensional shift," The Futurist interjected. "Change is the only Constant. Feel free to join it. The river flows with or without your consent."

"Yesterday, I believed the world was flat," the Priest returned. "I'm having trouble trusting the ground."

Reality was surely much more fluid here than on earthPresent. Or was earthPresent just a name… for what were actually quite different planets, all existing as each person perceived it to be. What a different place my world had become in the span of what might be considered a single day, much less a single lifetime! Yet the Priest knew, despite the proposed certainty of his convictions, the protests of his culture and intellect, that it was only different on the Inside.

"However much things may have changed," The Futurist reassured me, "it is still now o'clock. And now is always the right time to begin."

The Priest paused before the word "BECOME"… Surely, the only way to "become" was to walk right through the walls. And so he did.

The two inner-space travelers found themselves, next, in a room containing nine people, all sitting on toilets. Four men, Five women. Six of the nine sat fully clothed on the open toilets while looking through red plastic viewfinders. Two women and one man sat on the other toilets without apparel, and their thoughts were displayed just above their heads, as though projected from a hidden mind camera.

"Toilets, digestion. Let me guess," the Priest queried, "we've entered the Bathrooms of Inner-Space."

"Let's just say we're getting more physically oriented so that you get a better grasp on things," The Futurist said, with his eyes smiling brightly. "Will you be needing a viewfinder to see your intentions?"

"They used Red Plastic Viewfinders to see their Intentions."

And with that, he flicked an invisible switch in my mind which allowed me to see with vivid distinction the concerns of all those around me. The screen of the woman closest to me, for instance, revealed that in her inner-space world, she was staring blankly at an avocado.

"Something tells me," the Priest said hesitantly, peering over at the unclothed woman next to him, "Ce n'est pas un avocado?"

The Futurist replied again by smiling, as he levitated toward a very succinctly chosen spot, where he began to make rubbing motions as if he were holding a rag and was somehow cleaning his imaginary windows. Not that I doubted he was.

The Futurist chuckled and continued on with the creation of his latest magnum opus. "That's because you still don't know how to see," he said, once again interrupting my thoughts, which I was beginning to think was a bit rude.

"What do you know?" I thought silently. I could feel him laughing inside of me.

"Well," The Futurist said, "that is a ticklish relationship to figure out. Perhaps it's really you leading us through this." The Futurist lifted his walking stick into the air and prodded the sky for answers.

He was talking to me as much as he was addressing the Priest. I wasn't sure, myself, what we were supposed to be seeing. We were feeling a little disoriented. Perhaps we were looking for the future or better yet the past. On the Priest's mind-screen was projected an image of the back of his own head.

"earthPresent is no more," the Priest said to me. He was really getting disoriented, what with all the transformations occurring in such rapidity. It's very hard to see the basics when reality is shifting under your feet.

"*Walking on water is easy,*" The Futurist told him. "You are still on earthPresent. Even if it's not at all what you originally thought it was."

I stared blankly for a moment, but then became ignited with understanding. I began to illuminate.

A new door materialized on my mind-screen, and I watched as the knob slowly turned and turned. The Futurist smiled wryly at me. I was getting closer to where he was being projected from. Or something like that.

"A revolution is brewing," The Futurist proposed. "Do you know the source?"

I received his question in the form of a collage, as the door swung open with images, vibrations, and waves of the very distant past, beyond my own memory. From outside my body, I watched the screen that had appeared over my head, like the others in the room. I was not holding a viewfinder (thank God...) and The Futurist was there next to me, watching — or perhaps communicating — with one of my parallel existences, or future rooms. I could see the light shooting from his fingertips as he weaved some kind of elaborate tapestry.

"Look there!" The Futurist screamed, pointing behind me. As I turned around, the face on the Priest's mind-screen was unknown to me, yet I instinctively knew the man was somehow myself.

"Unicorns are as real as you," my voice was saying, "and just as visible. People are just short-sighted."

Around his neck, he wore a pendant of a sunbeam encircled by a ring of moons. The youth to whom he spoke shifted restlessly on the bench, but spoke with a calm older than his years.

"I can't see Unicorns," the youth returned, "but maybe being blind has that effect."

"Ce n'est pas un avocado..."

The man who spoke with my voice waved his paintbrush in front of the youth, whose eyes did not follow. As he realized the youth was blind, I was concurrently realizing that the man with my voice was a Craftsman of some kind. And I wondered if he, like The Futurist, could paint his own reality.

I noticed that in his other hand, he was holding a chisel. Something told me that the subject matter of his masterpiece remained a mystery, or was at least invisible to him at the moment.

"That's where you come in," The Futurist whispered from a yet unmateralized state. "Without him, there is no revolution."

Searching, the Craftsman sneezed from the anxiety of not knowing his own direction. He looked up at the clouds as if anticipating some kind of visitation. Glancing at his watch, he was getting uneasy.

"Nervous?" the youth asked.

"You're not so blind, after all," the Craftsman's voice replied, pleasantly taken aback. He smiled with appreciation at the boy, marveling at what a disquieting crutch living in a sightless state must be.

"People aren't really so different," the youth said slowly, "save appearances." He looked directly at the Craftsman, who thought he was looking just beyond him. He then kicked his walking stick high into the air, which startled the Craftsman.

"In fact," he continued, "I don't carry this walking stick because I'm blind, nor as a crutch. I know exactly where I am going."

"Why do you carry it?" the Craftsman asked, half-humoring the youth, half-humoring himself.

"As a reminder," he offered, "that life is just a walking stick."

"A walking stick?"

"The physical world," he clarified, "is the walking stick of the spirit... a tool to enact a vision upon."

The Craftsman looked up from the ground, and the blind youth was now an old man, completely naked, and giggling impishly.

"You didn't recognize me!" the old man playfully sneered, still with the child's voice, but watching with eyes that could clearly see Intentions.

"Futurist, it's you!" he shouted. "You're not dressed. You must put some clothes on! If people see you, you'll be arrested!"

The Futurist laughed without a trace of panic. He shook his naked body freely, and smiled with defiance at the uneasy man before him.

"No one can see me," The Futurist assured him. "You always take your experiences so literally. Really, it would do you some good to loosen up."

"We're not all accustomed to the atmosphere on your planet, Futurist," he said impatiently. "Well, who's responsible for THAT?" was the reply.

"It's amazing," The Futurist continued. "People here are so afraid of nudity. Do you think it's too revealing?" He opened his imaginary cloak, and then closed it tightly, as if to hide his inner-world from sight.

"You know, most people imagine beings from space to be very peaceful and dignified," the Craftsman scoffed. "If they only knew how sarcastic you can be."

"Yes, if they only knew we were really there watching, after all...and LAUGHING!" The Futurist held his ribs with the private delights known only to FREE men. "I mean, just you, waiting for me, looking up into the clouds like I was coming from UP THERE, somewhere."

The Craftsman sighed, pacing swiftly. "Look, there are things that need doing on my planet, as you know— so what's this all about? I need to get on with it."

"Your planet, my planet—all your divisions. Well, go right ahead," The Futurist said, "don't let me stop you." He opened his hands and proceeded to slowly evaporate into the fabric of the future.

"C'mon," the Craftsman said. "Enough games."

"It's actually you who are being so stubborn," The Futurist said, with a trace of seriousness. "I don't know how you get on."

"I do fine," the Craftsman replied. "Now what do you need?"

The Futurist began illuminating. A light shade of violet surrounded his person, and a tunic materialized, clothing his body. He looked into the Craftsman's eyes and communicated without words: 'YOU MUST PREPARE YOUR PLANET FOR A CHANGE. A GREAT NEW AGE OF PERCEPTION IS WAITING TO BE RECOGNIZED!'

"How do I accomplish that?" the man asked, trance-like and sounding unconvinced at his prospects of success.

"CHANGE THE SCHOOLS," The Futurist's mind energy replied, with his lips not parting, but emitting an enveloping warmth. "TEACH YOUR FUTURE GENERATIONS ABOUT THEIR ENERGETIC FIELD. TEACH THEM TO BREATH FROM THE PLACE BEYOND DEATH. EXPLAIN HOW THEIR MENTAL PROCESSES SHAPE THEIR REALITY."

"Is that all?" he said. "Is that all I need to do?"

"YOUR PLANET'S ENTIRE CONSCIOUSNESS IS POISONED BY ITS OWN INHABITANTS. YOUR SOCIETY IS STRUCTURED TOWARD BORING THE PEOPLE WITH SECOND-HAND LIVING; TURNING THEM OFF TO TRUE ADVENTURE. THEY ARE DISTRACTED WITH CONVOLUTED VALUES AND FALSE COMPETITIONS, GAINING FALSE REWARDS. YOUR PLANET IS A WASTE DUMP!"

"But they are addicted to these falsities," the Craftsman urged The Futurist to understand, mostly to save himself the trouble. "People can't handle mind nudity."

"IT IS ONLY A CULTURAL DIFFERENCE BETWEEN YOUR WORLD AND MINE. PEOPLE MAKE THE RULES THAT PEOPLE ARE SUBJECTED TO. ADJUST THE PARAMETERS OF YOUR CULTURE TO SUPPORT YOUR DESIRED FUTURE ROOM," The Futurist continued without a word. "WHAT YOU SEE AS REALITY STRUCTURES ARE MORE MALLEABLE THAN THEY APPEAR."

"Hmmm," the Craftsman boyishly grumbled, feeling still doubtful by the proposed plan. "The people will believe it is naive, Futurist. Very naive."

"SO IS BELIEVING IN UNICORNS," the Unicorn assured him. Her voice, solid as steel, made me drunk with pleasure. "JUST RELINQUISH YOUR DOUBT AND YOUR FEAR OF THE INVISIBLE WORLD. LIBERATION AWAITS. EVERY FLOWER OPENING IS SIMPLY SAYING YES!"

She shocked me by adding, "YOU'VE ALL BECOME VERY STUPID."

"Who can find freedom nowadays?" the Craftsman questioned.

"WHOEVER IS HIMSELF FREE," The Futurist replied. "IT IS SIMPLY A MATTER OF MAKING DIFFERENT CHOICES ON A PATHWAY TO SOME KIND OF OTHER."

The Craftsman stood staring blankly into the distance. The wind was noisy as it whipped through the avenues of the city, so dominated by man-made buildings too tall to see past.

At first, he could not remember why he was standing there. What was he doing?

Slowly he remembered he had been talking with The Futurist, who was now completely outside of view. Perhaps it had only been the wind.

"The Craftsman escapes his gray past."

Could he really change the ways of his planet? He knew he had the skills to construct the Architecture of Places Tomorrow. But the message, the words, the heart of such a place. From where would he get the substance to fill the great structure he was to create?

Misty-eyed, he gazed into the night sky. Usually, the answers of the stars could not be seen, drowned out from the lights of the city. But tonight, there was one incredibly visible star shining brightly. It was all alone—a simple product of itself—yet it held the greatest glory in the sky.

"It is now Time," he heard The Futurist's voice rattling eerily through the night, "to make a rendezvous... with a unicorn."

4:5 - "tHE rEVOLVING mIRRORS oF i"

The crowd was getting impatient. It had been billed as a one-time-only performance by the multi-dimensionally famous Galexia.

She was famous for her voice, which it is said, carries the very notes of InfiniteTime. Beauty itself was just a melody in her mind. Many planets were represented tonight, though as always, many would prove to be Short of Understanding.

"This performance is made available on a frequency which includes your current airspace," a voice called over the loudspeakers. "So, for once, don't change —or you may be rendered out of reach of this broadcast!"

The Craftsman was anxious to be a witness. The crowd began pounding in a rhythmic demand for Galexia. The excitement in their distant memories clawed at the walls of the moment, nervously exhilarated.

The lights dimmed, and the Great Lady of Time appeared, with her own emanating light to counter the darkness in the auditorium, a product of herself, spinning like the molecules at her core, a mirror of the spiraling galaxies. The haunt of her appearance was immediately recognizable to all, and many applauded simply by the sight of her. But the audience's true test still lay ahead of them: Would they know what they were experiencing?

Galexia stepped up to the glittering holographic microphone, closed her eyes, and slowly opened her mouth to sing. Most of the crowd strained to listen... closer and closer still. They could not Hear. Utter silence fell upon their ears as her lips moved. They became agitated, believing they were victims to some kind of hoax, rather than seeing that they had failed to perceive.

Static.

The Craftsman listened more closely, and at first, could hear only faintly. The seeds of sound multiplied in his awareness, and progressively came in more vividly, more distinctly, though the strength of the signal had remained constant. At first, all he could really hear was The Voice, but soon realized she was speaking in an old language that few understood. Invisibility, in any form, is a distinct way to communicate, and the fact that her sounds were present but went unseen by most onlookers only magnified his recurring sense that she was some incarnation or projection of the Unicorn. Reassurance of her specific form was becoming less necessary.

The spirals at her core reeled out through her voice, creating the most distinctive of echoing vibrations, which left imprints upon the walls.

The amount of light that crystallized in her tones opened all the doors in the Hall. Looking over the crowd, there were a select few who were receiving her transmissions, holding their heads in disbelief, allowing their tears to flow joyously without resistance. The sound was almost painful, like a terribly beautiful sadness. Yet still, tensions in the hall rose quickly, turning the concert into a small-scale riot. Some demanded their money back, but were reminded that they had not paid. The concert was given freely.

As the twinkling of the stage faded, the doors continued to open down the Craftsman's long internal hallways, melding with Galexia's frequencies as if by some sacred, energistic marriage. It was, in fact, a meeting prearranged by The Futurist before the Craftsman had ever been born, and which would exist long after his passing.

He touched the centre of his chest, and felt the symbol of the sunbeam encircled by moons, which was no longer a pendant but had now imprinted itself upon his flesh. Closing his eyes, he contemplated both the radiant sun and yet mysterious lunar presence Galexia had transmitted as a pathway to the stars. Be she witch, mere symbol, or a song itself, hers was a fluid state where static displays of color could become melodic, and shapes could become vibration.

But most importantly, he now understood what form his construction would need to take: Just like the unicorn, it would be an expression of art that cannot be seen or touched... yet one which, the more you experience it, the more you believe in it.

Rather than using stone and steel, the makings of The Future Room would be built on a sturdier foundation: music.

With a clear vision, the Craftsman walked boldly down the road before him, as his image likewise faded from my mind-screen.

"If a *Magician* is what you mean to be," The Futurist offered, "then you *must let magic* be your making."

He extended two fingers in the shape of an opening, as if creating an entry point simply by thinking of one, and then began flipping the fingers like a seesaw, swinging in space.

"Clearly, you mean to drive me insane by means of illogic," I heard the Priest say.

"Galexia's frequencies meld with the Craftsman's long internal hallways..."

"Ah, so it's logic you're after," The Futurist began cackling.

"Is that too much to ask for?" the Priest pleaded.

"Logic," The Futurist scoffed, "which uses a ruler to measure a mile, a yardstick to measure an eternity?" His gaze never did leave his own maneuvering fingers as he spoke, fascinated perhaps by the prospects of where such a masterfully invented doorway could lead. His eyes grew more intense as he began to ponder how he might walk through it.

The Priest's desire to escape was suddenly returning without warning. The future seemed too great a challenge, and his faith was waning. He was beginning to sense that some kind of leap would soon become necessary.

"You are a Dreamer, Futurist. An admirable illusionist, perhaps. But where is this all leading? Where is the practicality in all this dreaming?" the Priest demanded, trying to vanquish, finally, this Man of Questions, like a whisper in the back of the mind.

"You must never allow yourself to become so practical," The Futurist assured with an ease of words. "The urge for Practicality is responsible for the world's Very Most Dull Achievements."

He interrupted his own train of thought, checking the course of his immediate future by testing the direction of the Wind against his upright stick.

"So, the Winds tell me it is now time for flight," The Futurist said with a matter-of-fact nonchalance that stood in stark contrast to the Priest's sudden need for grounded reassurances. "And certain planes are crafted as a Passage... just for One."

Then he produced from his imagination the existence of a small reflecting mirror. "Take this with you." And as he handed it to the Priest, his image faded into a series of rotating illuminations.

The Priest raised his sword and began swatting at the unwoundable air, striking the poses of a warrior. He screamed helplessly against the oncoming sky, melting across forever.

I knew that the Priest was backing away from this brazen new landscape proposed by The Futurist. And perhaps, after all, it was in part my own fault. Was I failing to provide the necessary support? My many confusions were preventing me.

I wasn't sure how to reconcile the space between that part of myself that I saw developing in the Craftsman with the person I had come to believe I was, as the Priest of earthPresent. And I began to wonder how my sense of personal identity related to my changing perceptions of how to proceed. After all, there are a million blank books with "Revolution" as their title. But they will never become Real. Not without the words to fill the pages. Perhaps that was to be my role in all of this.

5:5 – "tHE mOLECULAR rEVELATION"

All of my ideas about what I knew and who I was had become like iron gates, which now stood between myself and The Future Room. But I sensed that only by casting off my Certainties, could I gain access to the Unknown. Simply in breathing, I could enter the necessary state for change: flux and balance. A sensation of waves raced beneath my toes. And suddenly, I felt how truly important it was to have gained the sacred knowledge of walking on water.

I could see my reflection mirrored in the waves, and somehow, I knew all at once that the answer to my search lay right here. This place I was seeking was not a place after all, nor was the Revolution an Outer Force.

My search was for a state of Being that would finally allow me access to this larger life filled with rooms without walls... and I thought of The Futurist's home, with its endless hallways, unraveling even into those spaces where there seemed to be Not. Only there in the Unseen, in the Invisible, could I learn what the Unicorn knew.

"The Unicorn was not the Colour of White, but the Colour of Light."

To manifest pure light—to do the work of the stars—I would have to become emptied of all resistances. I would have to let go of something, perhaps a fear, that had always told me I needed it in order to be "alive." By letting go of this illusion, I would not only live in a much more multifaceted moment, but redefine what it meant to be living. Maybe, then, even the stones...

I thought of The Futurist speaking from within the stone. Had it simply been a leap of faith that had allowed his transformation? And the Unicorn...she had said that Death would be my final illusion...

Kneeling upon the water, I caressed the shimmering image, as water dripped also from my eyes. I drank of myself fully, as if to kiss what could never be kissed, to believe so fully in the Unbelievable as to sculpt its living presence into form. From what other matrix of inspiration could a Unicorn possibly be borne but from the immaculate irrationality of a love such as this? A love summoned from the depths of such a personal and strange desire?

If the strength of this attraction could have broken through the unbearable walls of Time, I would have gladly melted away, into my own formlessness, for eternity. But apparently, some walls were not illusions. And the truth, as always, was greater than mere longing.

There was no way through. The only release was to be found in ripping myself away, just to quell the intensity. I gasped for air and the sky began to tremble, as blue storm clouds collected like tornadoes overhead. The Priest of earthPresent fell backwards onto the mountaintop, and released an awkward groan.

Looking out, he confronted the cost of his awe-inspiring view. I was lost to him, he thought. And what, then, of the Unicorns?

Concurrently, I realized that I had NOT lost myself in the separation, but had gained it. Our disruption produced some kind of chemical reaction in me. I felt expanded. It was like the same emotion of releasing, in the form of a flooding in. My whole cellular structure was spreading, yet I had no sense that it had an end. I was in the trees that looked over his figure and yet the rock that nestled at his rear. Perhaps "going inward" actually required reaching out… into everything. Perhaps, only then, could the Priest and I truly be as one. And only through that paradox, could we ever connect to the illusive ability we had searched so long to find: to speak the mysterious language of Light.

My disappearing visage appeared to him in waves. Reaching deep into my lungs, I showered wind down upon his tiny little body until he laughed unbearably from the exhilaration of the epiphany, revived by the thought that we would actually find our way to one another. Death was being conquered, and the Oneness of it all was no further than the tip of a Unicorn's horn.

The Priest stood up and danced gaily with the wind, as if I was the child he'd vowed never to lose, and had somehow lost. Now he could see the single-horned antenna angels, recovering for himself the emotional and invisible knowledge of true reality, like a future room in the mind, where a small light was always left on.

The sky began to melt overhead, as earthPresent began to vibrate. The separation of our physical form was causing, or allowing, this vast expression of our infinite variety to manifest so that it could experience itself in endless wonderment. My spirit was being infused within his flesh and his blood was giving breathe to my ghost.

Once again, I felt splattered across a vast canvas, being too much a part of the thing to be able to see it from the outside. A massive energy expansion was spreading rapidly across my Sky Planes and I knew without any question—the very structure of my planet was now changing its form.

This divine alchemy was somehow more than anything I could have planned or understood. And the force we were both so in love with was greater still than we, so it was easy to give over our wills, in complete trust, to the strange wisdom of the fates. Only through that trust, after all, had we ever reached such a miraculous state of union.

"Had it simply been a leap of faith that had allowed his transformation?"

The leaves pulsed with color and seemed to ring out like bells across our psychogenic fields. Here, everything was alive for the first time, and gently dying to its past. There was no solid ground, save the lustful flow of atomic impossibilities.

The Priest began spinning like the molecules at his core. Images of Unicorns gathered all around him in every direction as he followed that rhythm down a vast corridor, both tube-like and spiraling, as molecules and atoms always dance, traveling through inner-spaces.

His spinning reeled him further and further inward. His surroundings whirred and blurred until he became a tornado of colours rushing towards his centre. To keep from getting dizzy, the Priest found that he simply had to relinquish his sense of attachment to the physical world. Holding on would surely spell disaster for a journey so delicately maneuvered as this.

As the Priest gave way to his spinning, I knelt from within him, animated in this wilderness of consciousness. A small casket with the word "YES" carved at its core appeared before me. It glistened from a trick of the light, and somehow I knew that unlocking it would concurrently release me from my past and yet open all the doors to my future. But first, I would have to prove worthy of a great and terrifying gift... my own love.

As I reached to touch the chest, I noticed it was growling. Momentarily I withdrew my hand, but somehow could sense that the growling was my own, and that its unraveling lay not in some outer compulsion, but in a purely inner gesture.

It was as The Futurist had suggested it would be: At the end of Time, nothing else matters. All the approval, recognition and conditionality of planetary living dissolves, and you're left with only you on judgment day to accept or deny yourself into the Kingdom of your own deliverance. I was all alone with my Self, looking at my reflection and all I had ever been and done. Dare I embrace it all? Was I true? My hand trembled on the box as we prepared to look Inside. The mystery of life is not about our disbelief in Unicorns, after all, but about our disbelief in Ourselves.

All throughout my body, I felt the flower that the Unicorn had spoken of... She had said the flower opening was simply saying "Yes." As I did that, it allowed light of every colour to emerge from my core. I illuminated.

The Priest continued to spin into himself with greater ease, as my petals opened with the vivacious spectrums of any full-blooming peacock. Then, the energy redefined its essence into something that resembled the windstorm of a delicate butterfly wing, and the closed chest finally flew open.

The ebbing dream state stormed forward with one final explosive howl, and the Priest fell to his knees from the force of its aggression.

The wilderness peeled back toward a solid state, which was a relief for the Priest. The trees took on the form of trees, the sky was differentiating itself into an amorphous possibility above him, and I was no more than I had been... a whispering companion in his mind whom he could chose to listen to or ignore, though never again in quite the same way.

As the luminous clouds bellowed with countless swirling figurines overhead, I noticed that a new star had taken shape in the night sky. It winked as it glistened. And somehow, the knowledge of the existence of this single star caused a stirring in my heart that felt very much like falling... only toward the sky. And in its existence, a sign that the transformation of earthPresent was perhaps complete.

"Yes," The Futurist assured, "that's how Revolutions get their start. They occur first on the Inside."

The Priest looked at his watch, and marveled that it had lost all its numbers. The changes were not all on the inside anymore, he thought, but had leaked out into life.

The Unicorn laughed at his fancy, and said something he couldn't hear. But her intelligence washed through his Being, and his body moved to meet her meanings, swaying pleasantly from her intentions.

"His watch had lost all of its numbers..."

"Such is a Unicorn's way," The Futurist said, chuckling at the Priest's crude means of comprehension.

"My watch has lost its numbers," the Priest marveled again, not sure how to proceed, as I searched to understand my new planet. The dial was spinning of its own accord.

I felt the Unicorn whinny. Her uniform of light merely sparkled as she disappeared behind a bank of clouds.

"I won't be needing a watch," the Priest huffed, finally answering himself. "It is always beginning, and the direction to go in... still remains the same."

"Yes, and it's time you answered that one..." The Futurist said, "for both of us." Whereupon he turned, and began walking up a staircase that appeared under his feet as he moved.

Once he had vanished, I still heard footsteps. They continued on until I realized they were coming from behind me. When I turned, I saw a man approaching who I wasn't sure I'd seen before, but immediately recognized.

"Yes!" I said to the Craftsman, striding forward. It was one of those rare moments when an artist comes face to face with his Purpose.

And with outstretched arms, the Craftsman, the Priest and I passed through each other's visage, dissolving through the passageways of NeverMore and arriving, at last, through the doors of The Future Room.

Reaching the top of the staircase in his mind, The Futurist then emerged from the Tunnels of Slumber. And he awakens each day, just like this... to work a little more on his Masterpiece... the Creation of an Abstract Future which most closely resembles his Dreams.

FIRE.

THE BEAUTY BOMB

The Impenetrable Fortress

It was Galexia's mission and her fate to prove something largely not accepted as true on her planet. That the makings of the Organic Being, in its fabric of heart and thought, was much stronger and more sturdy than solid metals, and more persuasive than missiles. Poetry was on her side, and passion. In a simple act of grace, she was to show that the gentle whisper is louder than all the yelling in the world; the stammering of a romantic heart against the tanks of insanity and annihilation.

There were many rumors. Some theorized that the source of her great power was an energy gained from trusting over time in irrational moments and those subtle joys known only from the relishing of impractical diversions and silly games. She had somehow stored and transmuted these states of mind and harnessed their energy into a force that could beget universes with the slightest movement of her finger; to open gateways of time through the merest fluctuations of her throat.

The rebels would not be able to stop her for in her peculiar innocence, she was the true radical. Her lack of defenses and thus lack of walls became an impenetrable fortress. After all, how could you attack what was not there? How can you defeat an opponent unwilling to play and who can rewrite the rules just by thinking of them. It became quick knowledge that Galexia was not to be trifled with.

The Space Princess

Galexia was a Space Princess living on a planet being ravaged by war. But it was more than the destructive forces arising from a simple vying for territory, or a cultural collision against blind obligate worship. No, this was also a war accelerated by escapist hatreds and prejudices, escalating into an unsettling violence.

It was her destiny to penetrate the psyche of these combative rival factions with a shrewd resonance generated completely by her strange mental activity. It was a wavelength she was to transmit; one that would awaken the sensibilities of her world, Planet Alriita.

She was one hip chick with an enormous potency, though not in the realm of finance or firepower. But her prolonged sensitivity to oddities and eccentric undertakings had built up a depository of ignitable energetics composed of magical inclinations, guided by intuitions and instincts.

And accordingly, hers would be no ordinary line of attack. She would alter the destiny of nations with the singular cadence of her breathing patterns and crumble paradoxes with the flow of her garments. Of particular note, she was unafraid to take on the warring nations as an individual, without military might or political office. Just a woman with an idea, and a willingness to meld her mind with the history of time. It was only as a sole entity that she could access the exact states of furtive creativity necessary to alter the course of Planet Alriita's destiny, and overthrow the Bewilderment Plague that was so afflicting her people.

As only a very determined girl holding a mysterious proficiency could, she would hurl this web of emotion and molecular fields of psyche into space as a ball of energy with a transformative power to exert her will over the very structure of what others perceived to be Matter. In that, buildings would crumble. Colors would reconfigure. And so too, paradigms would shift from this simple outburst of interior decisiveness.

Far away from the battlefields, the boardrooms of war strategists, and the clamoring of corruptively choreographed media reportage, Galexia worked alone in secret in her small floating studio. It was a room of potions and incantations scribbled on small scraps of paper, that were tacked to the walls with needles and sewing thread.

She collected all her thoughts in this manner and interlaced their sentiment into a vibratory channel she would one day, in a single moment, open and deliver unto the lap of the world; an auditory blast of unimaginable patterns, a sentient embroidery.

A Basic Miscalculation

Another factor in the Equation of Planet Alriita's unruly predicament of fast bubbling tensions was the social deception derived simply from existing in a modern coercive world. This was a people inundated by cultivated ideology, designed to create false excitement, in an attempt to replace —and as a substitute for— real experience and natural pleasures, like thinking and creating, known as the making of culture. The reason for this distracting of the populace is that real self-exploration and its resultant arts, which fill life with beauty and purpose, don't readily speak a language of mass engagement. Failing to transfigure personal labor into some resultant gold was framed as a useless thing, a botched alchemy.

But to intentionally obscure the efficacy of personal magic! This disempowerment messaging would be highly indecent even for tyrants. So it was sent undercover, situated behind the facades of televisions, radios, and telephone touchscreens, entering directly into the optic and aural processing centers of any open and well-meaning mind that may lay in its path. Making its way into little chamber dens, across sprawling ballrooms, and into precious hideaways built for clandestine trysts with soft hands.

Such a climate of deception was itself worthy of battle and corrective measure. But it was indeed a hard dynamic to combat, due to its pervasiveness. While opinions may have differed across its various locales, the acquiescence to the demands of a basic miscalculation concerning the true nature of power was worldwide; the value of internal victories being overshadowed completely by a desire for access to better goods and services.

None of this was lost on Galexia, of course, who continued scribbling down each reflection into her notebook, which would become the initial base materials supporting her private revolution. She thought of cavemen carving their visions onto cave walls while she quietly sipped her coffee, looking out into the night sky...

The Beauty Bomb

It was a night like any other. Galexia gathered her robes and walked out towards the open field, only steps from her floating studio. She extended her arms forward as the wind gusts swirled through her hair. Her voice raised in energy, and she began to sing...

Hidden inside each of us, looming in whatever world, is the most powerful weapon known to mankind: the human heart. Though it stays locked in its chamber... centuries pass, the heart endures.

Galexia's experiment was to launch this unfathomable arsenal and set loose its power in a wave of color trajectories and beating pulse. This is the story of The Beauty Bomb, the most unexpected weapon in the War of Planet Alriita.

An incalculable component of her metamorphic artillery was a special awareness she held of the interwoven nature of all living sentience, connected like the energy veins in a leaf, biologically poised to spread her celestial impulses from being to being, in a chain reaction. Her long slender arms lightly fluttered in bird song vocabularies, ready to unite a divided world by a common core—just as five fingers spread from the human hand, or how five points of light refract from a star, in separate spires that can only function to best effect, when both autonomous and unified.

This cosmic integration came down to a simple matter of the heart. Down through the ages, the heart had been in a more or less perpetual state of closing; a survival mechanism for a time, but one that had outgrown its usefulness. The experiment of The Beauty Bomb necessitated the opening of this chamber that guarded the power of the planet's core and would be essential in fulfilling Planet Alriita's ultimate destiny— to engage in a powerful transformation of energy that would actually shift the nature of personal reality.

This is perhaps what vision is for. Simply in seeing as no one else had previously perceived, a wavelength opened. A past world could be set aflame. A new alignment achieved. A new organism. The beauty bomb could only fully be ignited by this rare limbic source carried by the human population, which if aligned just properly, could mirror the heart of the planet itself. Alriita's physical form would indeed change and expand to meet its new self-image.... One of love unfurled.

A little belief in the creative power of people was a necessary ingredient to the recipe, and just a little belief in the creative power of the universe.

EARTH.

A WORLD OF ALIENS

I was sent on a fact-finding mission by Intergalactic Council, an umbrella Control organization located in the same celestial quadrant as Earth. There had been a series of disturbing images intercepted by Earth media scans, depicting aliens as SILVER in color, which was brought to the attention of the Central Offices at "I.C."

Such alarming findings had proven to be warning signs of social decline witnessed before in other surrounding planets. Often in the progression of a species and civilization, we'll find an over-reliance on External Tools and Devices develops into a lack of Internal Balance, seeing even advanced races falling into species-wide psychic illness.

In the case of Earth, it is feared, this depiction of silver aliens was an indicator that reliance on their technologies had become overwhelming to the developing populace, and that the Earthlings were in danger of becoming a mechanized technology (read: cyborg) race, manipulated by the very inventions they had brought into existence.

Worse, could the Silver Aura Projection itself be a reflection of humanity's collective prediction of their own destiny... of becoming A WORLD OF ALIENS; a people *alienated from themselves.*

Such a predicament is regarded with great caution by the surrounding astral bodies, who do not wish for Earth to become a contagion threat as they develop their interplanetary citizenship, hoping that one day, this emergent civilization may be integrated with the Greater Kosmic Alliance. So it was, as a matter of intergalactic security then, that this voyage to Earth was initiated.

The mission [of course]: DEPROGRAMMING of the robot form.

This would require the construction of a small, unofficial culture, from which we could conduct our tests. The first surface-sensor download we received produced the troubling intel that the culture's shamans were not guiding forces in the soul work of the people, but were guided by sponsorships. Sponsorship which inevitably come from money sources, interested primarily in promoting WITH their money that which would continue the illusion of the value OF their money. Rather than a system of social validation celebrating true native expression, guided by internal impulses.

This tipped us off to at least one major root source of the Silver Disease.

We did of course have some advance trepidation in our planning, knowing we would need to tinker with something of sacred value on the planet. Indeed, we would be meddling with a kind of social oxygen: money.

Not that this was directly causing the mechanization. It was patently clear that what was happening really had little to do with money, but with ego. Not about money, but of listening to oneself. Not about money, but the result of a deprioritization of dreaming; a lazy conundrum of routines, distractions, and habits. A problem of perceptions, rather than access. But if there were too many strings attached to produce correct action among an otherwise free people, we would look at changing the hand behind the strings.

Such was our dilemma approaching the host ship, Earth.

We isolated a small stretch of territory where an accurate, successful experimentation could be made. Against all likelihood there was a small nook of largely unoccupied industrial development, with suitable and available housing, just outside the most vibrant of urban environments on the planet. It was here that "I.C." saw an Open Channel; a test case could be made from these raw conditions.

Williamsburg was almost abandoned even though it was one simple metro stop outside of the urban sprawl known to the host population as Manhattan, New York. This was a perfect situation for the realization of our investigation: situated just a stone's throw from enough cultural gluttony to ensure action could always be found at a moment's notice— all while maintaining a fashionable 'do without' attitude. A pretense that served our purposes... We didn't wish to be cruel, after all. We were simply utilizing something universally known to be eternal: temporary answers.

And the smoke screen of a metropolis suited all involved, as it's only in the most sophisticated, populated areas that one can find both access to large communication networks of people, and yet the ability to maintain an unchallenged anonymity.

Enter: ALIEN-SPONSORED PIRATE RADIO, which would be the voice of the silenced minority; those who would transmit our nonconformist perspectives, and which we theorized, could break the grip of the Silver Agenda.

The radio was to inform the twenty-block radius of this small test town. It was important for our purposes that the transmission source remain undetected.

And for this, Control provided us with an immaculate facsimile of normal Earth phenomenon, in the form of a well-coordinated flock of homing pigeons which constantly circled the skies above the low-rise buildings of Williamsburg, and which would seem nothing out of the ordinary. Except that THESE WERE NOT BIRDS, but a carefully constructed device which sent our pirate signals carrying subversive content to the people of the area, and which could be received only on localized tuned radios to 109.3 on the FM dial.

We were interested in the development of a community base with an exceptionally laid-back approach to experimentation, for only in this relaxed state of mental functioning could our subtle influences be received by the human population. The purposes of our mission required that the Billyburg inhabitants be especially receptive to the act of channeling. Only then could we be certain of the effectiveness of our techniques on this race to re-authenticate their experience. Much like a homing device ourselves, we would infiltrate the Earth consciousness and seek to equilibrate their psychic illness by returning them to a state of chill-ass astral elegance...or otherwise said, a condition of free-flowing source.

In our initial phase, local stores began to thrive, which were opened at odd hours, or at least kept irregular schedules. We saw to it that the ever-present clerk at Earwax Records would indulge the habit of working his entire shift standing barefoot on the street outside, and exclusively play Bob Dylan vinyl from 30 years prior; anachronistic stylings pouring through the front door and windows onto Bedford Avenue, rather than anything remotely current.

Instituting a fluid approach of neighboring businesses to adopt an "*Open When We Feel Like It*" attitude, instilled a profound emotional approval for anything *resembling* an uncommon experience. Quirkily unrelated merchandise would be paired for sale under one rooftop, such as a travel agency which would also sell futons and a large selection of used books. All arguably travel related, but with no logical practical crossover. This encouraged quiet vibes of wonder and a placing of playful mischief into hearts.

Facilitating the revaluing of a primal unprogrammed self in this town of Williamsburg —albeit in a somewhat controlled setting— would allow us to see if we could reauthenticate the human population on a larger scale. For this study to reflect a realistic possibility, the draw of personalities could not be sourced from a stagnant pool of influences, but local faces were to be replaced by an international character, with vast backgrounds and exceptional creative faculties.

The *Sound Mirror Pirate Radio* would transmit to this new breed of person, setting the mood for a sense of expanded relational dichotomies, enhanced risk-taking, and an increase in the complexity of perceptions relating to concepts of personal development and freedom.

As our story unfolds, it was entirely without warning, or any signs of media encouragement, that a strange clamor of excitement began to pull people almost inexplicably out of the popular circles of Manhattan and into the mysterious, abandoned warehouse environs of Williamsburg, Brooklyn. Of course, new arrivals couldn't afford the prohibitive costs of requisite handmade peculiar

art to adorn their walls, but almost instantaneously, the well-attended *$1 Art Party* sprung up as a recurring staple of cheerful exchange, while spearheading a 'can do' community zeitgeist, with its own power to define. It felt like an easy place to make a new start.

Indeed, it seemed to visitors that something unusual was "in the air", even though only weeks prior, they would have sensed nothing at all and not given the rundown area a second thought... though very possibly, many argued, this "something in the air" did have something to do with the active radioactive waste storage facility, severe pollution infractions, and sullying sewage odors that were remnants of the district's highly industrial past.

Also having endured one of the largest and longest running oil spills in the country's history, with an amoeba-like blob of toxic chemicals still present in the soil, Williamsburg had cancer rates 50 percent greater than the rest of the city. Next, the trees in McCarren Park contracted a strange disease and windows by the waterfront had to be sealed from the contaminant vapor toxicity of the area. It was, all in all, an environmental disaster.

But this too was necessary. The dangers of the vicinity assured rents stay affordable, and kept people more easily frightened away, who would've grabbed up all that desirably crummy housing we needed for our test case inhabitants. Pioneering spirits willing to take health risks for a strong creative opportunity and ample space for artistic experimentation would be drawn in, without the prospect of any immediate development on the horizon. True big money enterprises were afraid to invest in a region of such palpable upheaval, and what's more, there were no banks in the whole township. One had to walk to neighboring Greenpoint just to get access to cash, even if only for a subway token. Otherwise, you were stranded.

These roadblocks to practical living helped the fruition of our experiment enormously. With many deserted buildings, opportunities were plentiful for situational performance art events, and illegal rooftop screenings of experimental films, without need for printed invitations or pesky permitting. Word of mouth and pirate radio broadcasts created widespread and immediate awareness within this small, isolated stretch of blocks, that lay conveniently close to the L train subway, directly intersecting every transit line across Manhattan. From there, naked women with paint thrown down on them by Japanese action artists, with original film and sonic projections from the French underground, mixed with tap dancers who kept beat by means of lion whips, were to be regular features of the Williamsburg art scene.

Not to mention the opening of a used clothing store on Bedford and North 11, rightly known to locals as The Beacon— a home of delightful cheap-chic threads that cleared a path for novel shifts of identity, thereby binding the new sense of community literally by a cloth and shared fabric.

The flock to the area seemed to magnetically pull those who were young enough to be without need for structure in their daily living, yet old enough to be past the career-seeking phase that young artists often fall into, which blindly support the commodity reward system that had already so deeply retarded the psychic development of the Earth-race. Our test group would be people who had already evolved past these concerns, having come together to form lives inventively maneuvered and without attachment to 'being paid' and 'being credited' to acquire name recognition—or frankly, having any need for inclusion in the official culture whatsoever. But to build a haven to live within, just so it would exist.

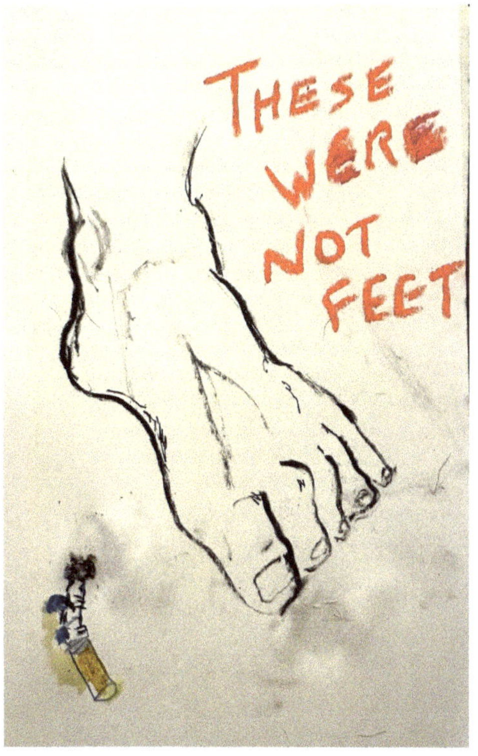

Yes, this would be a time of enjoying, rather than complaining about, whisky stained napkins at brunch, for the fine and good times they represented, of revelry experienced the night before.

Another inventive simulation we endeavored was to materialize a row of metal seats drilled into the broken concrete docks, a structural artifact left over from the area's defunct factory days, and which jutted away from the shoreline at the waterfront. This allowed residents to privately sneak to these hidden and unsanctioned spots, and look out across the water at the glittering skyline of Manhattan, without the impulse necessarily to go join it- but instead, to revel in gladness and contentment at being exactly where they were: on the outside.

We were pleased and impressed, as creating this subtle vibrational hypnosis was incredibly successful in facilitating our purposes. The field we projected over these blocks changed the psychographic makeup of the area, which quickly escalated from a virtual ghost town with empty subway platforms even at rush hour to a bustling, hip and happening urban mecca of activity only two years later, with stylish innovators and anarchists flittering across the metro station even at 3 in the morning. There were parties often formed at 5 am on weeknights without previous notice, debunking the patterns and expectations set up by the Silver Agenda.

All in all, the revolution we facilitated was a personal one; a quiet revolution. It was a revolution that occurred in people's lives, at an intimate level... the way they thought, valued, communicated, expressed, and even inhabited a moment. This much was changed. There were no grand protests and upheavals, violence in the street, political offices at stake. Just people in an environment with themselves. For that much, our efforts were a success, and the deprogramming and transformation witnessed, intense and total.

Before long, however, the neighborhood had stalemated, in part by having become too safe. After these five transformational test years leading up to the turn of the century— *1999*— many local newspapers and magazines began to hail the reign of the new avant-garde. But by then, young collegiates looking for the scene had repelled and displaced those original innovators who had been the substance of the community. As always, the very act of looking for the scene, in effect, had chased it away. Likewise, with many rents being paid for by distantly situated parents, the financial weight on foundational Williamsburgers had become too much, and the significant period of cultural development that the media was writing about had already largely ended. Revolutions rarely being funded activity.

The important thing to note, for our records, is that Williamsburg was a town.

It was a town like any other.

Williamsburg was a town like any other that, for the most part, never existed.

It never existed because it was an invisible town. A town that inhabited the same physical space as any town on a map, but which contained a coexisting intangible plane, which only some had access to.

The good thing about towns like Williamsburg, that never existed, is that they can reappear again at another time... someplace else.

They can exist anywhere. Providing, of course, that you're the type who could see them.

WATER.

CRYSTAL CITIES RISE FROM THE OCEANS

I t all started from a dream. I was swimming up a waterfall. I recall now the sensation of the water cascading down all around me, while my arms moved in firm strokes. Deliberate, determined, delphinic. I was gliding upward against the current without any strain, and as I hit the top, my body swayed peacefully, in the same way a boat bobbles in a bay.

"I swam up a waterfall."

My voice let out a soft *"ahhh…beautiful"* and taking account of where I had landed, sat basking in a misty haze. The glow of a soft halo could be felt along my facial features.

Awakened, and with only the memory of the dream as to how I got here, I managed to steady myself against a rock, feeling the lines of my fingers greeting the lines of the boulder.

Looking down the shoreline of that rambling river, I knew only one thing about where these waters were headed: that I didn't know.

But it became immediately clear that the building of a craft would surely be needed. Having no means of constructing a boat, I envisioned what one would look like and so it appeared.

I named it Isis, after the great Egyptian goddess, for it was she that gathered all the scattered pieces of Osiris and put him back together again. Just as I must now put the pieces together about who I am, and how I got here.

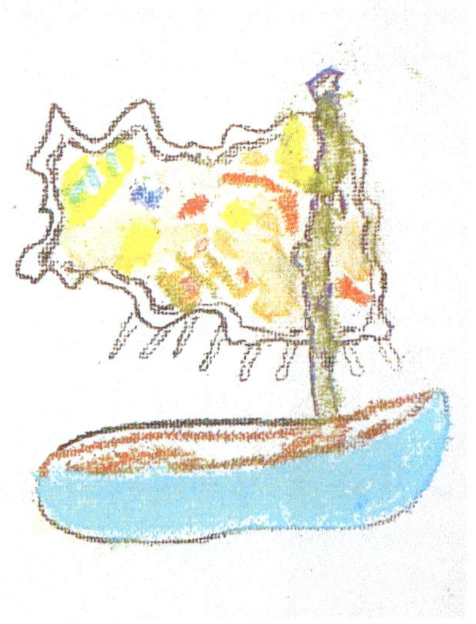

"I drew a scarf as a sail."

The cloudless sky started to drizzle, so I grabbed a fallen branch that was seemingly waiting expectant against the boulder, and placed it into the readymade socket at the center of the deck. I traced my fingers against the air and quickly drew a large canvas scarf I could throw over the mast, tie to the hull, and fasten tight.

That'll do, I thought.

Sailing into tomorrow I traveled, but not without questions. I didn't know how I knew I could draw this sail into being, and I looked at my hands with some wonder. Who was this person who could make something from nothing?

I was charmed by the hum incanted by the water, which sang a song both calming and yet befitting a gallant journey. And this humming brought cheer, and a feeling that I was not quite so alone.

Even with these few initial successes achieved since waking, which should foster some confidence, it does not appear to have swept from my mind the inevitable confusions one gets wrapped up in; like whether you are on your game, making your mark, or lost at sea. Certainly, some who think they're on their game are lost at sea, while some believe they are lost, but are not so at all.

I suppose there is uncertainty even for those who are touted as being the very best at whatever skill! After all, those I knew with the best hands and touch never pursued the path of a masseuse. The funniest didn't go into comedy. The best singers had better things to do than entertain. This must leave us all with some very serious doubts about claims of anyone ever being "the world's best" ANYTHING. I guess that's also why the idea of who the best is, always keeps changing too. Because none of it is likely true.

But for now, I knew I was shielded from the rain by my scarf sail. And sometimes that is enough to know.

So, I listened to the river humming its song and was grateful for the mountains that conveyed strength and resilience, watching over me from such a high majestic place. An altitude where falcons and other raptors fly. Even if I didn't know who I was, I could hear my thoughts… and those were the thoughts of someone.

It even seemed like the mountains were thought-amplifiers and reflectors, which magnified my ability to hear my own ponderances, including the really quiet ones. But it also seemed the mountains contained a riddle. Because they hum too. In fact, all those layers of solidity are comprised of motion and vibration, in precisely the same way a song is vibration. In some way, no more solid than oxygen or light. And that is very heavy…

The gentle trading of melodies and harmonies in the humming of cascading water and mountain terrain seemed for an instant that they were really the same. And so I must be like them too, both sturdy and fluid.

The rain now had cleared, so I stood up in my boat, and leaned the mast to the left, letting the sun address my face.

I closed my eyes and felt the warmth, and yet the cooling effect of the wind in my hair.

A few select leaves did not survive the breeze, falling along the riverbank, as the borders of the water widened into an increasing vastness. I suppose an opening can feel threatening, but this was an expanse that heightened my mood. I felt almost a rapture. This helped me realize that feeling rapture all around and inside yourself doesn't require being any special kind of person. It just requires paying attention.

Looking at my hobbyish primitive boat, I saw it too needed an expansion. Not just to provide greater control over my destiny, but to somehow make contact in this vast world. I started drawing more scarves as sails. I thought, if I made enough scarves, maybe my craft would be visible from a hundred miles away, from all the way in space! It occurred to me to draw not only canvas scarves, but silk ones too.

Not that making MORE is any great thing. Many could try to convince themselves they were a great artist, or worse a professional one. Simply by producing a great many things over a great many days. But art for the sake of producing objects doesn't tell us that. It may only mean one is a neurotic. But making art as a means of producing the kind of person you can be. That is really something.

If it were only a matter of quantity, I should wish to count instead how many nights of sunsets had been traveled through. And what was their character? Their consistency? How did the color smell on a cool night, if we could know such a thing. I think many kinds of animals do know.

I leaned over now to place my hand in the river, as if to gather information. I noted an increased velocity of current, picking up speed. Whereas I began my journey against the flow, the waves now seemed to have shifted from a build and break to a glide and gush. And as manually using my arms to adjust the sails was growing tiresome, I drew some skilled and nimble birds who were only too happy to steer and take over as skipper of this trusty vessel.

Shifting attention allowed me to look directly up, instead of in front and around. It was that beautiful time of dusk where even though there are still pretty details of light, you start to see stars appearing. There is just a magic there, and you can imagine why some people want to be stars. A thing that seems eternal and pierces the darkness, and appears to do it in style. But that feeling fades as you find the light in your own life and become that radiance, it would seem.

"I drew a ladder for me to climb, so I could better understand the sunset..."

I became still and beaming for a moment contemplating this, and watched the pretty silk colors receive light and blend into the hues and tones of the sky, as it is when the sun drops below the horizon to produce curious atmospheric effects.

As the sky darkened and the air became chilly, I drew a little stone firepit and a flame, which gently came alive and crackled. I could not recall my own life enough to know if I had ever experienced fire on a boat surrounded by water, but it is a beautiful thing. And so I did this for four nights in a row after each sunset. If you learn nothing else from sunsets, it occurs to me that they would be lessons of design. Because beauty without design is still beauty, but less so.

While I still didn't know who I was, I understood something new about myself, in that I knew it was important to appreciate beauty, and I also knew that this came easy to me. Some people, I imagine, do not find the beauty in things with great ease. And so, I also saw that this appreciation was a way of just being thankful. And again, that not everyone is. Because some want to be stars. And at that moment, I suppose, something... is not enough.

It was a similar lesson when I was eating. I drew a small plate and then sketched the most beautiful donut to place upon it. The kind of donut that deserves to be placed on a really beautiful plate. It is about honor, I think. Even if it's for a simple thing, such as a confection. Because it deserves the dignity of a setting and to be featured, and in return, tastes better the more you dream of it. That's what I call a friend.

"Donut as partly eaten friend, under spotlight."

But where dreaming is concerned, and certainly much could be said of this, nothing resembles a dream more than a sunset.

I've had so many observations on why that's so. Like the humming I heard from the water was somehow magnified by those colors in the sky. And I don't think that was a false impression. What's more, I saw that the designs in the sky were melodies; they moved like notes and played like chords. I think this is likely why even listening to music in your car sounds better when there's a sunset to view.

As the river made its transition to the ocean, I noticed a new effect. The sunsets were bigger and I was no longer only seeing segments. And so I understood myself further. That sometimes we only see part of ourselves and magnify that portion like its everything. But we're more than our moments. Our problems. We're more than our strengths and our weaknesses, and callings. We're also our laughter, and often we can't hear that at all.

I was relieved to see that there was a bigger realm than whatever we inhabit, because being confined to a boat can limit one's view. And to explore these optics further, I drew some paper and crayons to begin marking down my studies for more scrutinized inspection. I took note of the light shifting through the trees and branches, and the reflections in the waves of the water, and the branching and outstretch of clouds across the sky. I came to observe patterns, then began drawing patterns, and in that, the ability to understanding their dynamics.

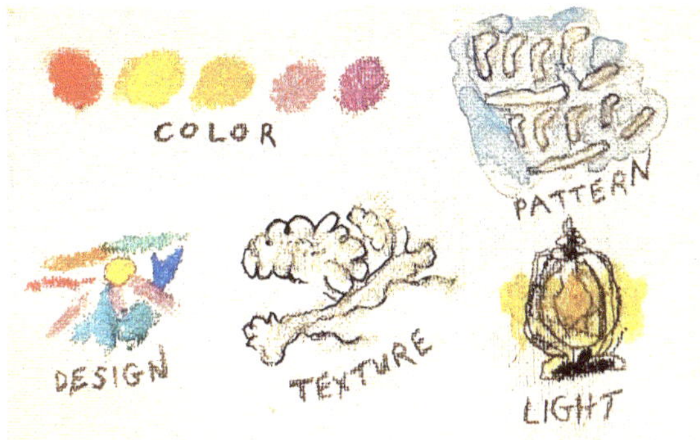

"Dynamics of a Sunset (Deconstructed)"

One thing to know is that patterns repeat. They have order. And the best patterns create order that reveals something magnificent and feels like proof of something. They bring comfort, because they are solid in their arrangements. And are made up of colors that are themselves every bit as solid as stone, even when they move across the sky, like water.

That is to say, I really did feel a sense of comfort at this point in my journey, because I was seeing myself reflected in all these phenomenon— and I felt not so much a stranger.

I didn't know my name but I knew something of what I was. And also felt part of something, because all of existence was right here, humming. Even in my nights, there was music, from the water, from the fire, from the birds. Each in their own overlapping pattern and yet delivered in their own separate rhythm. And that meant I could also be many things at once.

"The sunset taught me how to design a scarf with an abundance of style."

In this instance, it meant I was content but also hungry. Not for food, I could draw that anytime. It was a hunger for home. All this drifting was fine, but I wasn't a river, just in motion, nor was I the sky, which was everywhere...

To remedy this, I decided to take a new action— one to hurry! I would put all my knowledge and everything I learned into getting home! Color, pattern, texture, design— they would each move me forward.

To increase my speed, I resorted to more scarves! And MORE SCARVES! Bigger and increasingly ornate scarves, worthy of the ancient regality of Isis shimmering across time, and yes, in real style.

I wasn't a humble rickety boat anymore. But a three-masted cruiser with increasing scale for private opulence. I would tell you more, but it would no longer be private.

"Then I drew the birds a bit larger to handle all the extra scarves... Even a crayon bird needs help sometimes."

Which reminds me to mention... memory and time are also both fluid and solid. Time is in motion always, but you really know when time is of the essence. When it's your moment to arrive. When the bell rings, and for no one else but you.

We string our moments together, and from just basic elements —of soil, stones, fire, water, breezes, and thought— we build worlds that invent the future we live in. It rises right before you, fully formed. As if waiting all along for your arrival.

My craft shook as if awakening, with the water suddenly becoming impassioned. I grab hold of the rail. Swirling pools of rising bubbles gather around the ship, and the hum is magnified by turbulence. The birds drop to sit at my shoulders, ready to relinquish their skippering, and hand me back control of the sails. This brought me calm. With just an initial adjustment, my winged passengers and I were serene within the vessel. Like watching a storm from behind a window, in a warm safe enclosure.

Massive structures capable of holding every measure of weight, jettison toward the sky. Glistening, towering, immaculate. The water parts for their emergence, and I watch in awe as Crystal Cities Rise From the Oceans, made of amethyst and sandstone. Brilliant corridors seen through stained glass sheets, tall as skyscrapers. My days behind me, as if pre-written by the future, seem to lead me directly to this point of entry, just as the waterfall had.

My ship, which receives but also delivers me, has penetrated the harbor.

Approaching the port slowly,

                drops the scarf sails down,

                            kicks the stern,

and the bow grazes the dock.

Postlude: Past as Prologue...

A Time Capsule

This special *30th Anniversary Edition* of "The Future Room" includes snippets from the live performances of the music recordings that the book's content was originally adapted for. Enjoy this peek-a-boo into another Time!